Read•A•Picture
RHYMES & STORIES

By Burton Marks

Illustrated by Paul Harvey

SMITHMARK

# GRISELDA THE WITCH

In a land far, far away, there was once

a witch by the name of Griselda.  lived

in a  near the edge of the forest.

Unlike most witches,  was good and

very kind.

Every morning she made soup out of

and and gave some to the monsters

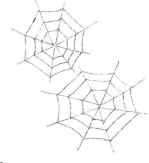

who lived in the  .

Sometimes would do magical things.

She delighted in changing into .

But her favorite trick was to change

into , and into .

's days were busy, but sometimes she was

lonely with only the  in the

to keep her company. Then one day a good witch

named Brunilla moved into a  nearby.

 was very excited. That same

afternoon she invited Brunilla to come over

for tea and  and  .

The two witches had a wonderful time.

They rode their 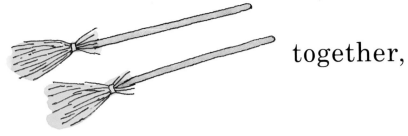 together,

they cast spells together, and they laughed and

told funny stories.

 couldn't have been happier. "How nice

it is to share things with a friend," she said.

THE BIRTHDAY WISH

If today were my birthday, I'd really like...

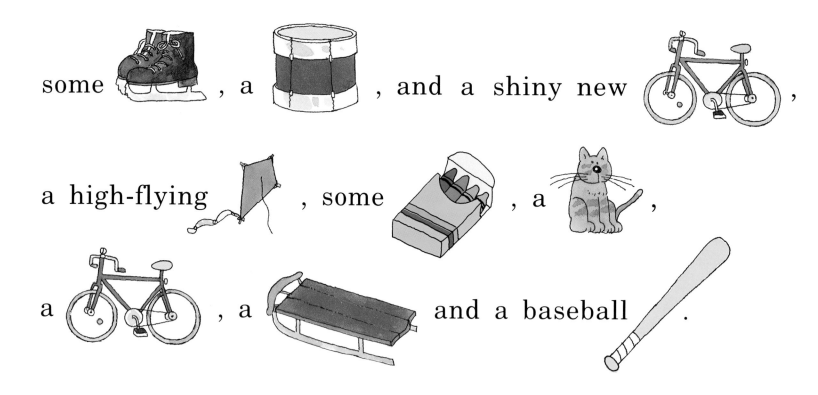

some ____, a ____, and a shiny new ____,

a high-flying ____, some ____, a ____,

a ____, a ____ and a baseball ____.

I know that my birthday is **6** months away,

but I couldn't wait till the very last day

to tell you the things that I'd really like.

By the way, did I happen to mention a

?

ELWOOD BROWN

Elwood Brown is a sad-faced  .

His face is painted with a frown.

But it's not a  says Elwood Brown,

it's just a  that's upside-down.

DID YOU EVER

HUNGRY PETE

A troll I know whose name is Pete
can't seem to get enough to eat.
He gobbles everything in sight
to satisfy his appetite.

He eats the most unusual things

like ⬡ 🏀 and 🪀 strings,

and coats and 👟 and 🧦,

flower 🌸🌸 and cuckoo 🕰️,

🍌 peels and old tin 🥫,

plastic 🪣 and frying 🍳.

When Pete the troll has guests for dinner
he serves them sand and gravel stew.
And if you are very nice to him
he might have you for dinner, too!

BEDTIME

Can't I stay up longer?
Just **10** more minutes, please!
We could play a game, and
I'll say my ABC's.

Can I have a  of milk?

Will you listen to my prayers?

Will you read me the 📖 about

Goldilocks and the 🐻🐻🐻 ?

Will you bring me a ,

some  and some 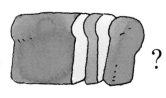 ?

Will you see if there's a

hiding underneath my  ?

Can't I stay awake

just **5** minutes more?

Can I have another 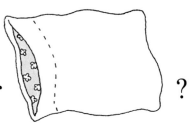 ?

Will you open my 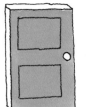 ?

Can I have my

and my 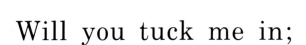 ?

Will you tuck me in;

will you kiss me, too?

If you sing me a song

I won't make a peep.

Please turn off my  .

I...think

...I'm

asleep.

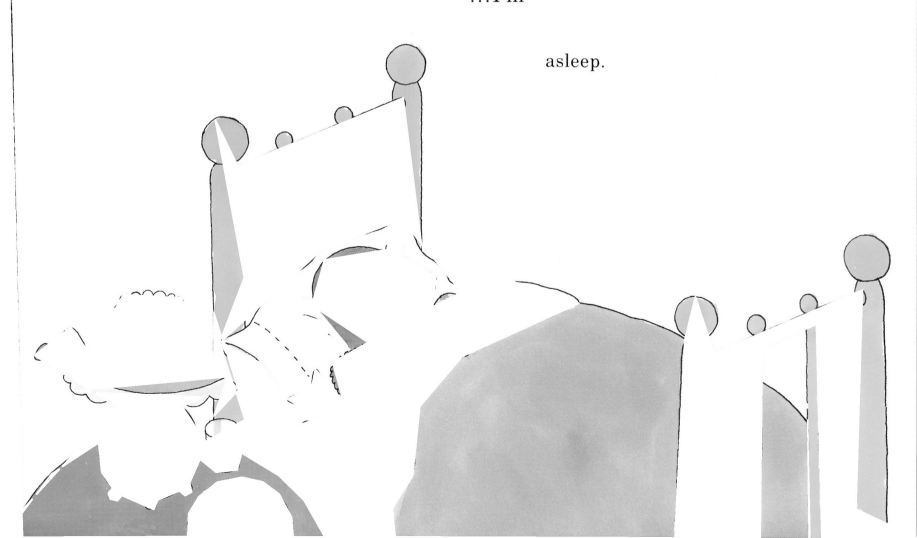

WHERE IS MY TEDDY?

I'm looking for my Teddy  .

He's hiding in my yard somewhere.

I found my ⬤ , my ◆ , my 🚢 ,

my 🚗 , my 🦆 , my dolly's 🧥 .

I even found my rocking  .

Why can't I find my Teddy  ?

Can you help find my Teddy Bear?
I know it's hidden here somewhere.
My other things are hidden, too—
I just found them...now can you?

I'M NOT *THAT* HUNGRY

I'll eat anything you give me.
Every meal will be a treat,
except for one thing I must tell you
that I simply will not eat.

I'll eat  and liver pancakes,

raw 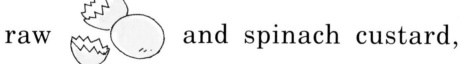 and spinach custard,

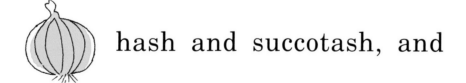 hash and succotash, and

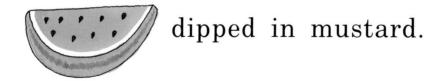 dipped in mustard.

I'll eat mush and  pudding,

turnip greens and creamed 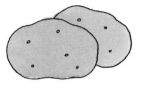 ,

 peels and pickled eels,

artichokes and green  .

Oh, I'll gladly eat all these, and

even olives stuffed with 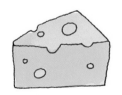 .

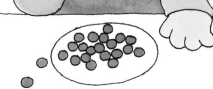 But I beg you on my knees—
please...

don't give me any 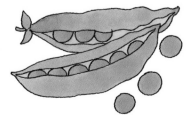 .

T's it, t's all,

U are at the end.

Close the  & gin again!